This book belongs to:

....

H 00 7121899

Schools Library Service

To Billy and Zadie,
my huggable little friends

Big thanks and big hugs to my editor
Emma Layfield and designer Paula Burgess

HODDER CHILDREN'S BOOKS
First published in Great Britain in 2020 by Hodder and Stoughton

Text and illustrations © Zehra Hicks 2020

The moral rights of the author-illustrator have been asserted.

All rights reserved.

HB ISBN: 978 1 444 94997 1   PB ISBN 978 1 444 94998 8

3 5 7 9 10 8 6 4 2

Printed and bound in China

Hodder Children's Books
An imprint of Hachette Children's Group
Part of Hodder and Stoughton
Carmelite House, 50 Victoria Embankment, London, EC4Y 0DZ

An Hachette UK Company
www.hachette.co.uk
www.hachettechildrens.co.uk

PUG
HUG

Zehra Hicks

Hodder
Children's
Books

Hug?

Pug, do you want a hug?

Why don't you ask Cat?

Cat? Hug?

No, thanks.
I don't
like hugs.

Hmmm,
you could try Hamster ...

Hamster?
Hug?

**Never mind, Pug.
Rabbit likes hugs . . .**

Rabbit?

Hug?

Sorry, I'm a bit busy right now.

**Don't worry, Pug.
Who else could you ask?**

Fish?
Hug?

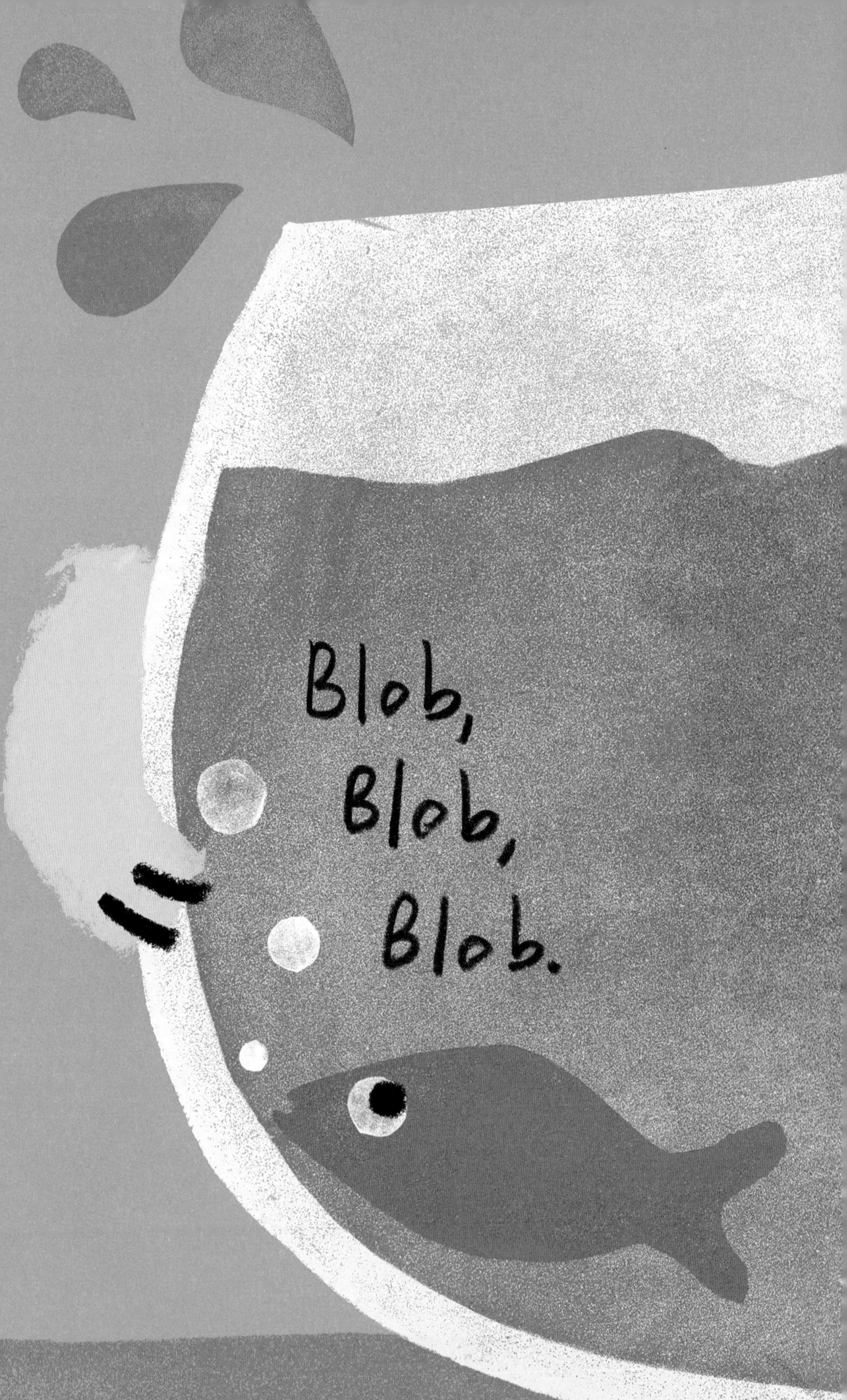

Ah, tricky!

**What about Parrot?
Parrots love hugging.**

Parrots? Hug?

"Pretty please?

Funny
Puggy!

Funny
Puggy!

Funny
Puggy!

**Keep looking, Pug!
Someone will want a hug.**

Guinea Pig? Tortoise?

Mouse? Frog?

Spider? Chick?

ANYONE HUG?

Don't give up, Pug!

I'll give you a hug.

Watch out, Pug!

Help!

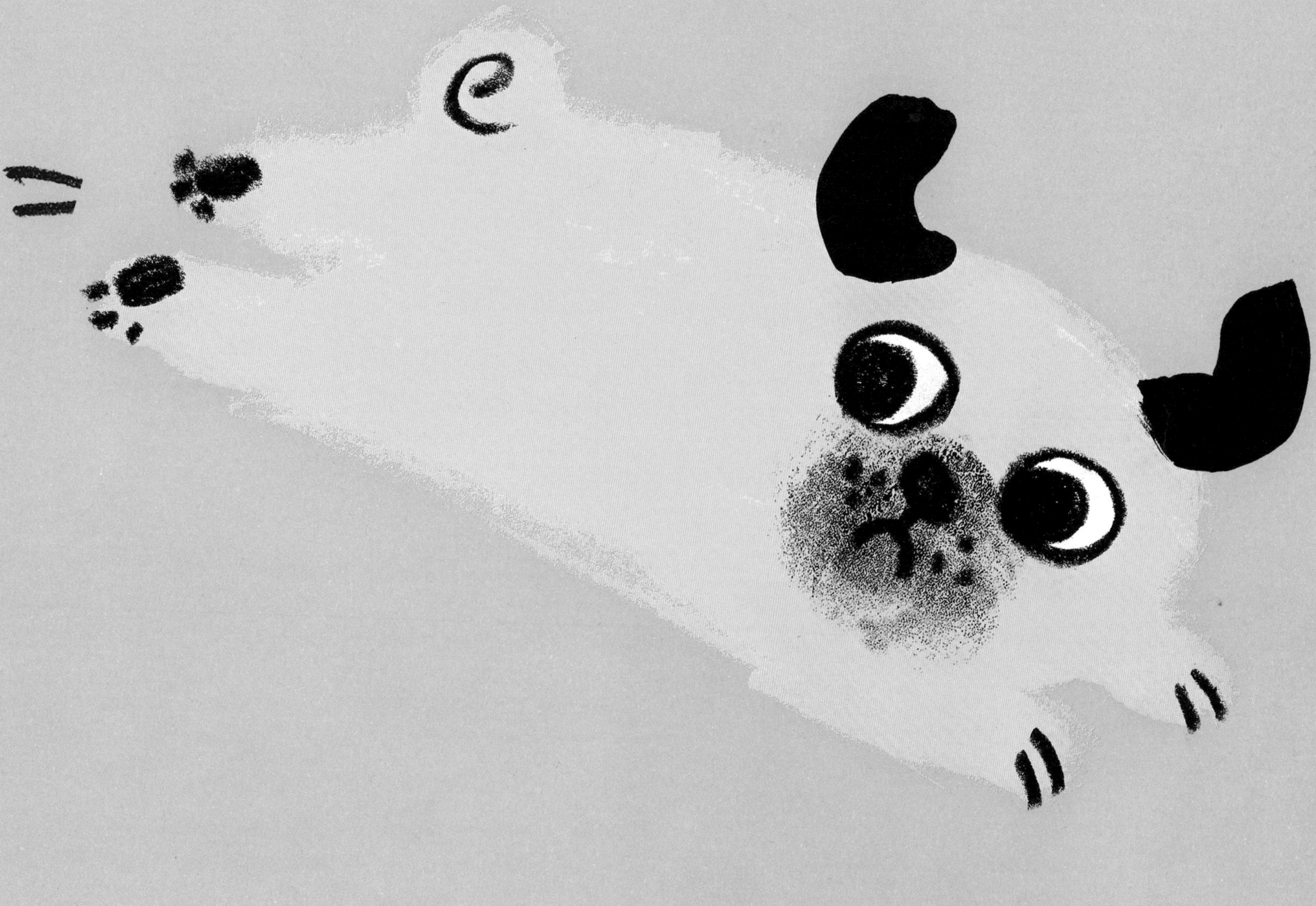

**Phew!
You've found
the perfect hug.**

Now everyone have a
pug hug!

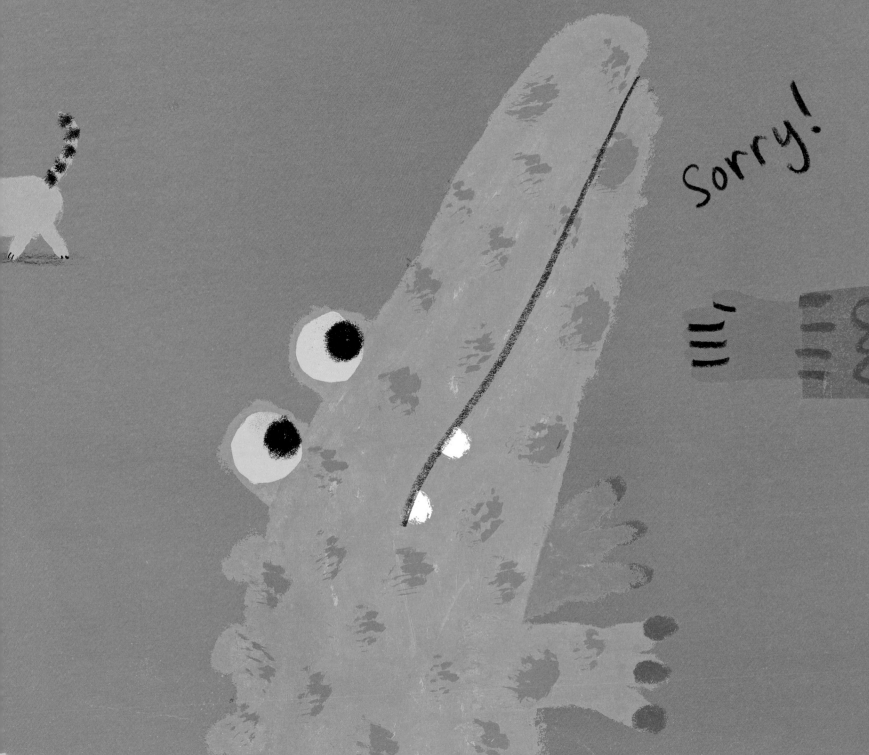

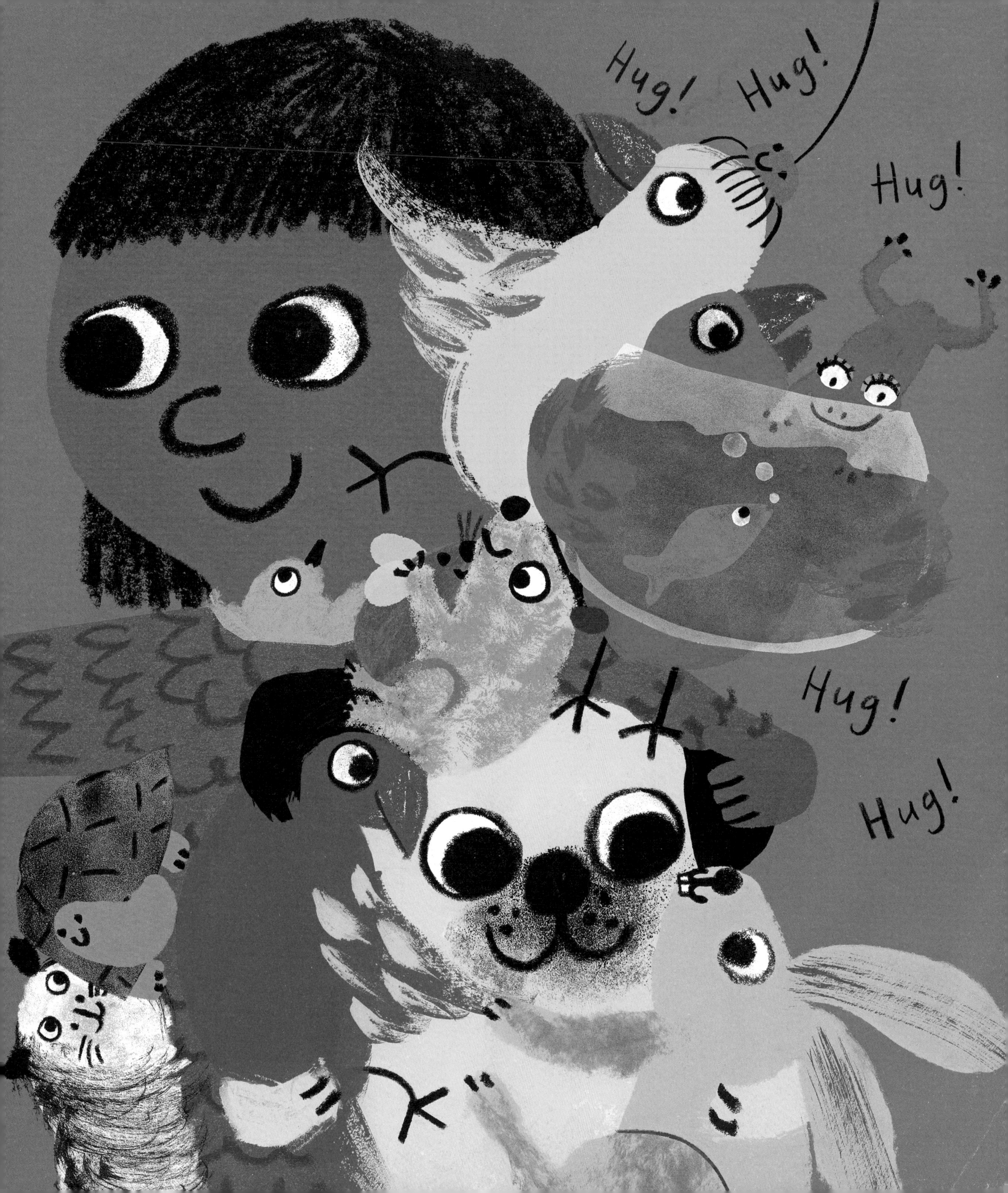
Hug! Hug!
Hug!
Hug!
Hug!